The Bear Whose Bones Were Jezebel Jones

Bill Grossman

pictures by Jonathan Allen

Dial Books for Young Readers New York

To Pat Brennan, Dan Norton, and Rick Shoemaker–B.G.

To Marian, Alasdair, and Isobel–J.A.

Published by Dial Books for Young Readers
A Division of Penguin Books USA Inc.
375 Hudson Street
New York, New York 10014

Text copyright © 1997 by Bill Grossman
Pictures copyright © 1997 by Jonathan Allen
All rights reserved
Designed by Nancy R. Leo
Printed in Hong Kong
First Edition
1 3 5 7 9 10 8 6 4 2

Library of Congress Cataloging in Publication Data
Grossman, Bill.
The bear whose bones were Jezebel Jones / Bill Grossman ; pictures by Jonathan Allen.
p. cm.
Summary: Jezebel Jones dons the skin of a bear after he removes it to go swimming,
and she can't take it off until some animals at the zoo figure out a way to help.
ISBN 0-8037-1742-3 (trade).—ISBN 0-8037-1743-1 (library)
[1. Stories in rhyme. 2. Bears—Fiction. 3. Humorous stories.] I. Allen, Jonathan, ill. II. Title.
PZ8.3.G914Be 1997 [E]—dc20 94-31907 CIP AC

The art for this book was prepared using gouache and isograph pen over
a pencil outline on watercolor board.

Carrying a bathing suit, snorkel, and fins,
A bear trotted down to a lake for a swim.

But before he jumped in,
He took off his skin
To rinse off his bones.
Skipping along came Jezebel Jones.

"Wow!" she said, "look at this skin."
She picked it up and climbed right in
And zipped it up and scampered away
To see what her friends at school would say.

She was sitting there quietly in one of her classes,
When her teacher said, "Jezebel?" and put on his glasses.
"You seem a bit hairy . . . and beary . . . and scary!"

He picked up his papers and ran away fast.

And so did the rest of Jezebel's class.

Jezebel Jones moseyed on home.

"Eeek! It's a bear!" her mother cried.
"Don't worry, Mom, it's just his hide
With me inside.
I'm his bones,"
Said Jezebel Jones.

But her mom didn't hear what Jezebel said.
All that she heard was "GRRRRR" instead.

For every time Jezebel opened her mouth,
Bear talk—just bear talk—was all that came out.
And in bear talk everything sounds like "GRRRRR."
Her mom ran away, for it frightened her.

"I'm much too scary," said Jezebel Jones.
"I'd better return this skin to its bones."

She went to the lake to look for the bear.
She looked and she looked, but the bear wasn't there.

"He's gone," she said. "Well, I'll take off his skin
And fold it up neatly and leave it for him."

But . . . oh, no! . . . she couldn't unzip the bearskin.
(Of course not—only bears can unzip THEIR skin.)

So off she went to look for the bear.

Jezebel Jones looked everywhere.

In a fox's lair.

In the stall of a mare.

In the hole of a hare who was scared by her stare.

But the bear wasn't there.

She looked in a field full of men playing cricket.

She looked under leaves in a very dense thicket.

She stepped from the thicket onto a street
And was given a ticket by a cop on the beat,
Who showed her a sign with words clear and neat:
"NO BEAR FEET ARE ALLOWED ON THE STREET."

"These aren't my feet," said Jezebel Jones.
"I'm not a bear. I'm only his bones."

But the cop didn't hear what Jezebel said.
All that he heard was "GRRRRR" instead.

"And a warm, hearty GRRRRR to you too, little bear,"
The cop replied as he left her there.

Jezebel continued her search for the bear.
By and by she came to a fair,
And while she was there,
She gave such a scare
To a ticket taker
And a basket maker
And a clown with a funny red nose
That they jumped right out of their clothes
And scurried away in their underwear,
Followed by everyone there at the fair.

Jezebel threw up her arms in despair.

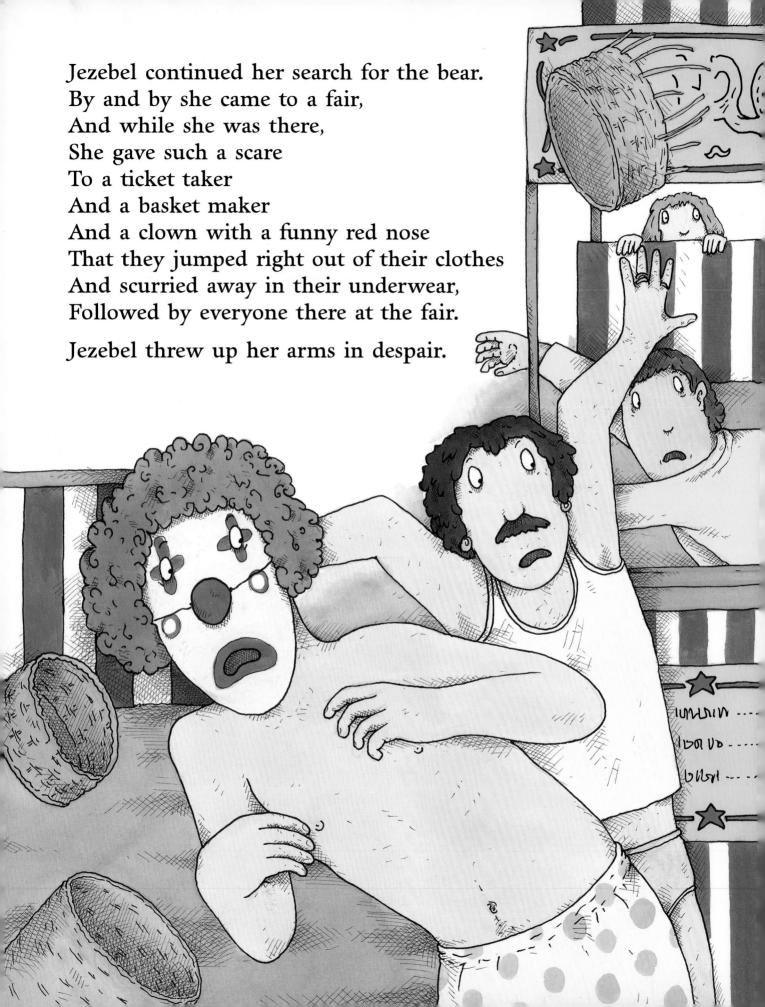

Poor Jezebel, she was very distressed,
So she lay in the grass by a ballpark to rest.
Plunk! A nearsighted umpire sat on her chest.

"This bearskin rug's a bit lumpy," he said,
As he rested his elbow on Jezebel's head.

Jezebel tickled the umpire's feet.
"It's alive! It's alive!" the umpire shrieked.
And he leaped to his feet
And ran down the street.

Jezebel sat, feeling down on her luck,
When a whole bunch of girls drove up in a truck.
"You look sad, little bear. Are you lost from the zoo?
We're headed right there. Do you want to come too?"

"I'm not from the zoo," said Jezebel Jones.
"I'm not a bear. I'm only his bones."

But when Jezebel spoke, it sounded like "GRRRRR,"
And the whole bunch of girls believed she said, "Sure,"
So they grabbed her arms and lifted her up
And carried her off to the zoo in their truck.

"What's your name, little bear? You must be new,"
Said the friendly animals at the zoo.

"GRRRRR," Jezebel Jones replied.
Then she lifted her paws and forcibly pried
The mouth of the bear till it opened so wide
That everyone there could see down inside.

"EEEYOW!" the animals screamed in surprise
When they looked in that mouth and saw Jezebel's eyes.

Away ran the zebra. The monkeys did too.
But the elephant stayed, for he knew what to do.

He reached out his trunk and pulled a dog near
And whispered something into his ear.

The dog jumped up and ran around,
And sniffed the air and sniffed the ground,
And sniffed the road and sniffed the lawn,
And sniffed the woods and then was gone.

Soon he came running to Jezebel Jones.
Clenched in his teeth was a bundle of bones.

A bundle of bones that was dressed rather cute
In a snorkel and fins and a bathing suit.

The bundle of bones unzipped the skin,
Let Jezebel out and climbed right in.

Then the bear trotted off with his skin on his bones
And waved good-bye to Jezebel Jones.

Jezebel waved to the bear and went home,
Where the only skin Jezebel wears is her own.